Contents

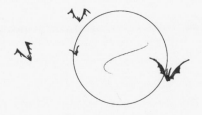

Chapter 1
Wilfred the Bold

I'm sure you've heard of Count Dracula, the evil vampire who could turn himself into a bat. The creepy fellow who always wore black and enjoyed a neck of warm blood more than anything.

Yes, everyone's heard of Count Dracula. But do you know what he was like when young? Before he grew tall, swept his hair back and hung around in graveyards? Not likely! Because until now, the story of young Dracula has been a secret – a secret that I (a very nosy writer) have at last unearthed.

But before I tell you this secret story, you must learn about life at Castle Dracula before young Dracula was born. Listen up. This bit's important.

Once, far away in Transylvania, there were two rival vampires. One was Count Dracula. The other was Baron Gertler. The Count and the Baron lived in tall black castles on opposite sides of the valley.

Far below the two castles was a village.

Late every night, village bloodmen – like Transylvanian milkmen – rode up to the castles with bottles of fresh blood for the Count and the Baron. The bloodmen collected a cup of blood from all villagers aged between 10 and 80. The villagers had no choice. It was a very old law.

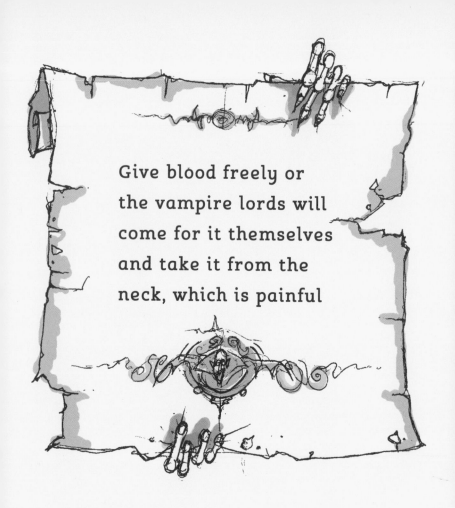

Give blood freely or
the vampire lords will
come for it themselves
and take it from the
neck, which is painful

Now, for a long time, neither Count
Dracula nor Baron Gertler had children to
follow in their bloody footsteps. But one year,
the Count brought home a wife. And the year
after, Countess Dracula gave birth to a son.
They called him Wilfred.

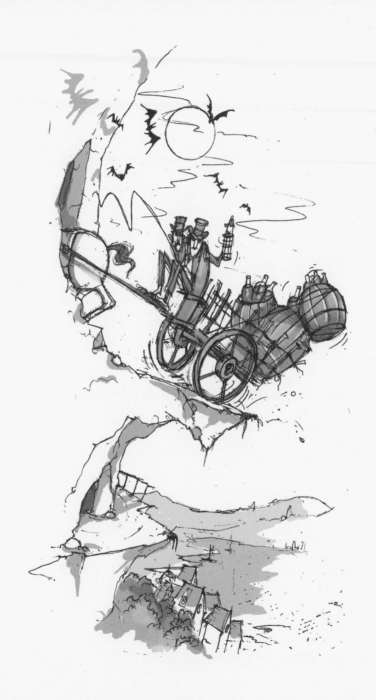

When Baron Gertler heard that the Draculas had a son, he turned green with envy. Then he turned himself into a huge bat, flew to the castle and snatched the baby from his mother while the Count clipped his toenails in the bath. Then he flew off with the baby.

The Countess rushed to save her darling son, but as she reached for him, she leaned too far out of the window and tumbled to her death far below.

The Count jumped dripping from the bath and when he saw what had happened, he gnashed his vampire teeth, turned himself into a bat and flew after the Baron. The Baron escaped, but the Count saved baby Wilfred and took him home.

Two nights later, the Count sneaked into Castle Gertler before the Baron was awake, and hammered a wooden stake into the Baron's mean old heart.

Twelve years passed. Count Dracula was now half the vampire he had been. He couldn't turn himself into a bat any more. He never went out at night. The villagers didn't fear him. The bloodmen didn't deliver. He had to drink the blood of the rats that ran around the castle.

One gloomy midnight, the old Count gazed out from his high tower. He saw the ruin of Castle Gertler across the valley. No one had lived there since the Baron's death.

"Ah, those were the nights," the Count said, a tear in his eye.

He missed having an enemy. He missed going out for a neck or two of human blood whenever he wanted. There was no one to talk to. No one that mattered. It was no use talking to Wilfred. They had nothing at all in common.

"Are you all right, Father?"

The Count jumped. He hadn't heard Wilfred come up the stairs. "What do you want?" he snapped.

Wilfred was a kind lad – and he was worried about the old vampire.

"Would you like a bowl of toad and tomato soup, Father?"

The Count scowled. "No, Wilfred, I do not want soup. I want warm blood, bit of froth on top, no sugar. If you cared about your poor old father you'd go down to the valley, drag a villager out of bed, and drain his blood into a jug for me."

"But, Father, you know I hate doing that," Wilfred said.

The Count sighed. "One day," he said, "you'll be head of the House of Dracula. I

wouldn't be surprised if the first thing you do when I'm nothing but dust is put flowers everywhere. You're not a vampire, Wilfred, you're a wimpire!"

These harsh words stung Wilfred. He so wanted to be like all the Draculas before him. Why was he different? He went to his room and got sadly into his coffin.

Wilfred fell asleep. It was never easy for him to stay awake at night – another thing that upset his father. The Count was old-fashioned. For him, vampires should sleep in the day and be up all night, sipping the red stuff.

But for Wilfred the good thing about sleeping at night was the dreams. Night dreams were sweeter than day dreams. Tonight he dreamed that he didn't have to live in a cold, gloomy castle or file his teeth before getting into his coffin for the night.

Nor did he feel like a wimp for liking milk better than blood. He had a cow of his own. In the dream he could lie under her in the straw and dung, and drink fresh, warm milk to his heart's content.

In this wonderful dream, Wilfred ran through open fields in the sunshine, singing at the top of his voice. The sunshine didn't make him cry out in pain when it touched his skin, like it did in real life. In the dream, Wilfred was who he wanted to be.

But when he woke, the dream vanished in the gloom of the castle. He heard again the Count's unkind remark – "You're not a vampire, Wilfred, you're a wimpire."

"I so want Father to be proud of me," Wilfred said, determined to prove that he was a true vampire after all.

All that day, Wilfred waited indoors, hiding from the sunlight. Then, as night fell, he slipped out of the castle. He took with him a jug to bring back his father's favourite drink – human blood.

Wolves howled as Wilfred went down Bram Hill. He trembled, but on he went, down into the valley. He had no idea that his life was about to change – for ever.

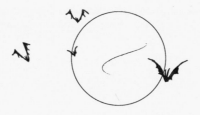

Chapter 2
Followed!

Wilfred planned to go to the village. It was night and the villagers would be asleep. With any luck he would be able to creep into cottage after cottage and take all the blood he needed from the necks of his victims. It was a suck and spit job.

Stoker Wood was on Wilfred's way to the village. No one went into Stoker Wood at night unless they were a vampire or very stupid indeed.

There was no wind but still the trees in
the wood creaked. Unseen birds fluttered
above Wilfred's head. Small animals scuttled
at his feet. Bigger beasts moved in the dark,
their sly eyes glowing.

Wilfred gulped. He gripped his jug and on
he went, deeper and deeper into the wood.

After about 15 minutes, Wilfred heard a
small, regular sound behind him.

Padda-pad. Padda-pad. Padda-pad.

Wilfred paused. The small, regular sound
paused too.

He began walking again.

Padda-pad. Padda-pad. Padda-pad.

Wilfred started to run. The small, regular sound sped up too.

Padda-padda, padda-padda, padda-padda, pad.

And then? Wilfred tripped over and fell flat on his face.

And another sound joined the first.

Pant-pant-panta-pant. Pant-pant-panta-pant.

The hair on Wilfred's head sprang up, and so did he. He sprang to his feet, climbed the nearest tree and perched on a big branch. His heart thudded as he looked down. An enormous wolf stared up at him, licking its hairy lips.

"Fooled you, Mr Wolf!" Wilfred jeered. "You won't have me for supper tonight!"

He clapped his hands at his own cleverness. As he clapped, his elbow bumped something. Something big. Something with hot breath and yellow eyes. Wilfred stopped clapping. He peered into the dark.

On the branch was a large, inky shape. What was it? Was it some wild animal hungry for a tasty snack of boy meat?

"Waaaaaaaaaaaaaaaaaaah!" went Wilfred as he toppled off the branch and into a pile of leaves. At the very paws of the wolf. The wolf growled – and pounced.

But as the wolf pounced, something odd happened. It should have torn Wilfred apart and swallowed his heart in one gulp, but it didn't. After the wolf pounced, it lay there, on top of Wilfred, moving neither tooth nor muscle, ear or paw.

Wilfred lay under the wolf for some time, eyes shut tight. He expected the worst. But when the worst didn't happen, he opened his eyes and gave the wolf a gentle prod.

"Mr Wolf, are you OK?" Wilfred said. "Nice wolfy."

The wolf still didn't move, so Wilfred eased himself out. The wolf just lay there. This was no surprise, really, because ... there was an arrow in its back!

The wolf was as dead as a rusty doornail.

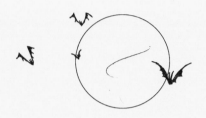

Chapter 3
The Night Hunter

Wilfred looked around. Nothing moved. Nothing made a sound.

"H-h-h-hello?"

No reply. Not a word. Not a whisper. Not a burp.

Wilfred's spine tingled. The silence and stillness scared him as much as the wolf's *padda-pad*, *padda-pad* and *pant-pant-panta-pant*.

So he kicked up his heels and ran for his life. As he crashed through the wood he felt that something was running with him, something he couldn't see. Something wild and dangerous, something that could kill him as soon as look at him.

And then it was gone, and Wilfred was alone again.

Owls hooted – *oo-hoo, oo-hoo* – and Wilfred came to a halt, wishing he was back home, snug in his coffin.

But then he remembered his plan to prove he was a true vampire and make his father proud. He must get to the village.

But which way was the village? With all this mad dashing about, Wilfred had no idea. He wandered this way and that, but he never came to the end of the wood.

Every now and then there was a movement ahead of him and Wilfred swerved to avoid it. Then, a little later, he would sense a presence in the dark and swerve to avoid it too.

All of a sudden Wilfred smelled something very odd in that haunted wood – roasting meat. He peered between the trees and saw a campfire's bright flames. He crept forward till he came to a clearing. In the clearing sat a boy.

The boy had his back to Wilfred. He sat on a log roasting a squirrel over the fire. The squirrel looked as if it was getting nice and crisp. Wilfred realised he was very hungry. He licked his lips. He could almost taste that squirrel.

But then he cursed. He was a vampire. Vampires only eat cooked meat when there's nothing living to sink their teeth into.

Wilfred looked again at the boy. He wore
a long black cloak with the hood thrown
back. An easy matter to sneak up, bite the
boy's neck and sip some blood to take the
edge off his appetite. Then he would squirt a
little more blood into his jug and go on to the
village for ...

The jug. Where was it? Wilfred looked around. He was sure he hadn't dropped it or put it down, but he no longer had it and that was a fact.

So now what? Perhaps the boy in the clearing had something he could use. Wilfred couldn't ask, because some of the blood he planned to take home was the boy's. Perhaps if he took just enough to weaken the boy he could find a container, then squirt some more of his blood into it. Good plan!

Wilfred crept across the clearing until he stood behind the boy. He got ready to sink his fangs into his victim's neck. But then the smell of tasty squirrel pinched his nose. 'Oh, why am I a vampire?' he thought. 'I would much prefer leg of squirrel to neck of boy.'

"So what are you waiting for?"

Wilfred jumped. The boy had spoken and turned to look up at him.

"It's quite clean," the boy said.

"Wh-what is?" Wilfred stammered.

"My neck. Washed it only last month. But you'll have to be faster than this to bite me!"

"How did you know I was behind you?" Wilfred asked. "How did you know what I was going to do?"

"Eyes in the back of my head," the boy said. "And if your teeth had come within a nip of my neck you'd have needed a dentist. What's it all about? Think you're a vampire, do you?"

Wilfred stepped over the log. "I don't *think* I'm a vampire," he told the boy. "I *am* a vampire. My father is Count Dracula!"

This took the boy by surprise. "Count Dracula is your dad?" he said. "But he's my hero! I'm a night hunter because of Count Dracula!"

"Night hunter?" Wilfred said.

"Someone who hunts by night. I'm good at it. Always have been. As soon as I could walk, I wanted to stay out all night and sleep all day like the Count. My parents used to curse Dracula. They said he set a bad example to young boys."

"Don't your parents mind now?" Wilfred asked, sitting down on the log.

"Not since the night of the storm when lightning struck a tree near the house," the boy said. "It crashed through the roof and flattened them in their bed. I was out at the time – hunting."

"How sad," Wilfred said.

"Oh, it could be worse. I can go out whenever I want now." The boy looked at Wilfred. "What's your name?"

"Wilfred," said Wilfred.

"My name's Smirk," said the boy, smirking. "Like a bit of squirrel?"

Wilfred shook his head. "Vampires don't eat cooked meat."

"That's a shame," the boy said. "I cooked it just for you."

"For me?"

"I was expecting you. In fact, I led you here."

"Nobody led me," Wilfred said. "I walked whichever way I wanted."

"Mostly you ran," Smirk said. "And every now and then something made you swerve and go another way. That was me."

Smirk tore a leg off the squirrel and offered it to Wilfred.

Wilfred was so hungry that he took the leg and, vampire or not, sank his teeth into it. It was the best thing he'd ever tasted. He saw Smirk watching him.

"Don't you want any?" Wilfred asked.

"No. I have no taste for dead flesh."

As if to prove this, Smirk grabbed a mouse as it darted by and popped it in his mouth. The little hind legs and tail stuck out between his lips, twitching. He crunched hard. The little hind legs and tail went limp. Smirk spat them out and chewed up the rest.

"You dropped this," Smirk said next.

Wilfred stared. It was his jug, the one he'd lost. "How did you get this?" he asked.

"You dropped it when you climbed the tree to escape the wolf."

"You saw that?" Wilfred said.

"More than saw it," Smirk said. "Where do you think the arrow came from?"

"If that was you, then I owe you my life."

"It was and you do," Smirk said. "Eat up now."

Wilfred ate up. The squirrel was so tasty, and the fire so warm, that he grew sleepy.

"Feel free to take a nap," Smirk said.

"I can't. I have to go to the village. I must fetch something for my father," Wilfred said.

"The night is young. Plenty of time for a nap and a trip to the village and still be back before dawn. Go on, have a little nap."

Wilfred couldn't resist. He curled up next to a big log and soon he was sleeping like ... well, like a log.

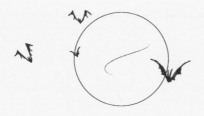

Chapter 4
Smirk's Gift

Wilfred's eyelids felt warm. He opened them, and was almost blinded by sunshine. He flung his arm across his eyes.

"Oh no, the sun!" he cried in horror.

Smirk stood nearby, his hood pulled up over his head. "It's not done you much harm so far."

Wilfred lowered his arm and, to his surprise, the sunlight did not hurt him. He'd never been out in the day before. He had never felt the sun on his face, or seen it dance on the back of his hands.

"I don't understand," he said. "Father says daylight hurts vampires. It's even worse when we're older. Then it turns us to dust. All my life he's told me that only normal people can survive the daylight. People like you. Boring Normals, he calls you."

"Is this what you call normal?" Smirk said.

He tugged the hood back. His face was as pale as death, his eyes as red as cherry tomatoes. He looked very ill.

"I'm allergic to sunlight," Smirk said. "It gets worse every year. When I was little, I stayed out at night and indoors between sunrise and sunset to be like the Count. Now I have to, like it or not."

"Why aren't you indoors now?" Wilfred asked him.

"Because I wanted to see what the sun would do to a real vampire."

"But it might have really hurt me," Wilfred said. "And you would have just *watched*?"

"I was curious," Smirk said, pulling his hood up again. "I've never met a real vampire before. But the sun doesn't seem to hurt you at all – unlike me, and I'm just a farmer's son."

"Do you realise what this means?" Wilfred asked, excited. "All these years we Draculas have shut ourselves away in that gloomy old castle when we could have been out and about. We could have chatted to the neighbours, had picnics, gone boating on the river! I must go and tell Father!"

"I thought you had something to do in the village," Smirk said.

But Wilfred was keen to be off. "Goodbye, Smirk. Thanks for killing the wolf and cooking the squirrel. Perhaps we'll meet again one day."

"Can I come with you?" Smirk asked.

"No, no," Wilfred said. "Father only welcomes visitors who want to donate blood. That doesn't include you, does it?"

"No," Smirk said, firmly. "Look, I just want to see him. He won't see me, I promise."

"You don't look well enough to walk all that way," Wilfred said.

"Who said anything about walking?" said Smirk. He lifted his arms and his long cloak fluttered about him. Then his feet left the ground.

Wilfred gasped. "Boring Normals can't do that! Even I can't do it, and I'm a vampire. Father's tried to show me many times, but I just can't get the hang of it."

"I've been doing it since I was little," Smirk said. "It's a gift, I suppose, to make up for being allergic to sunlight. Here, take hold of my cloak."

Wilfred took hold of the cloak. Then he and Smirk were rising through the trees. This was all so odd that Wilfred forgot his jug again.

Soon, the wood was a bright carpet of leaves beneath them. Wilfred's amazement turned to joy. He laughed and looked at Smirk, but his new friend's face was hidden by his hood. For a moment, the hood looked just like the head of a monstrous bat.

"Are you ready?" Smirk asked. "Then off we go!"

The cloak folded about Wilfred, flapped like great black wings, and then they were flying – yes, flying! – towards Castle Dracula.

Chapter 5
A True Vampire

Smirk said nothing until they were near the castle.

"I've always longed to visit this place," he said from deep within his hood. "Where do we find him, your noble father?"

"He'll be asleep," Wilfred said. "That's the window of his coffin-room up there."

"The shutters are shut," Smirk said.

"Shut against the light, that's all. They're not locked."

They stopped on the wide window ledge. Wilfred pushed the shutters back a little.

"There," he whispered.

Smirk pressed an eye to the gap in the shutters and saw his hero snoring in his coffin. The same gap let in a shaft of light, and it touched the Count's hand.

"He'll be so angry if he knows I've brought someone home," Wilfred said. "You'd better stay out here."

"Stay out here? You forget, I'm allergic to the sun."

"Oh, all right, go in," Wilfred said. "But don't make a sound – and hide yourself."

Wilfred opened the shutters a little more and Smirk jumped in, silent as a cat, and padded across the gloomy room.

While Smirk hid behind a heavy curtain, Wilfred entered the room. But he was so keen to speak to his father that he left the shutters open. The sunlight followed him in as he went to the coffin and shook the Count gently.

"Father," he said. "Great news! It's not true that direct sunlight harms vampires. We can go out whenever we want!"

The Count frowned in his sleep. He stirred. His lips drew back to show two sharp teeth at the corners of his mouth.

"Who disturbs my slumbers?" the Count growled.

"It's me, Wilfred. Father, wake up. You don't have to sleep in the day any more. Look, I'll show you."

The Count sat up and scratched his hand where the sun had touched it. What nonsense! The sun harmless? Had the boy lost his mind?

Wilfred ran to the window and flung the shutters wide. Sunshine flooded the room. The Count, in his elegant black pyjamas with 'C.D.' on the pocket, scrambled out of his coffin.

"Wilfred, close the shutters!" the Count shouted.

"It's all right, Father! The light won't hurt you!"

The Count stepped forward, intending to slam the shutters shut. But the sun fell full upon him and all his energy drained out of him. As the golden glow bathed him from head to foot he drooped, and the wax in his hairy old ears melted and dribbled out.

"Oh, foolish boy!" he wailed.

Wilfred stared. "But why does the sun hurt you and not me? I'm your son, your flesh and blood. It doesn't make sense."

"Oh, but it does," the Count said. "I've suspected it for years. Close the shutters. I have something to tell you, Wilfred."

But Wilfred was too excited to think about shutters. "What, Father, what?"

"Remember the story I told you of when you were a baby and Baron Gertler turned into a bat and flew off with you?" his father asked.

"Yes," Wilfred said. "What of it?"

As the sunlight ate into him, the Count grew more and more wizened. His cheeks shrivelled. His jaw stood out like a bent shovel. The bones of his wrists and elbows looked like knotted string.

"I followed the Baron," he gasped. "He had a head start on me, but I saw him carry you into a farmhouse before he escaped. He paid for that night's mischief later. Oh, how he paid!"

The red gleam came back to the Count's eyes as he remembered how he had defeated his old enemy. But then his eyes dulled and his chest caved in. "The shutters, Wilfred, the shutters."

Wilfred slammed the shutters, but not properly. As he returned to his father's coffin-side, one of them swung slowly open and light filled half the room – the half where the drooping Count was sprawled against his coffin.

"Go on, Father," Wilfred said. "What happened then?"

"By the time I reached the farmhouse," the Count went on, breathing hard, "the night was almost over. The sun would soon be up. I flew into the house to scoop you up – and found a cot with two babies in it."

"Two?" Wilfred said, startled.

The Count's splendid black pyjamas turned to rags in the golden light.

"In his haste," he went on, "the Baron had dropped you in the cot, next to the new child of the house. I had to decide – and fast – which of the two babies was mine."

"But surely you knew your own son," Wilfred said.

"All babies look the same," the Count snapped. "I had to make a choice before the sun rose and destroyed me. I grabbed

the one that seemed to have my nose and ...
Wilfred, I hate to say this, but ..."

"You brought the wrong baby home."

"It seems I did," the Count said.

"So, I'm not your son?"

"No. Sorry, Wilf."

"Can this be so?" Smirk, the night hunter,
stepped out from behind the curtain.

The Count's brittle jaw almost shattered
upon his chest.

"Who's this?" he demanded.

"His name's Smirk," Wilfred told him.
"We met in Stoker Wood. He saved my life
and gave me roast squirrel to eat. He's your
biggest fan."

"More than a fan," Smirk said, from the shadows. "My mother often told me that I changed overnight when I was a baby, but she never dreamed that I might have been exchanged for her real son."

"Exchanged?" Wilfred said. "You were exchanged for me?"

Smirk's eyes were bright red and the teeth at the corners of his mouth looked very sharp. "It explains everything. My allergy to sunlight. The fact that I can fly. My taste for live flesh. I'm not a Boring Normal. I never was. I'm the true son of Count Dracula!"

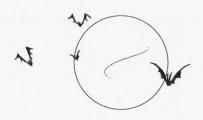

Chapter 6
Dreams Come True

Smirk risked the dreadful sunlight to dart from the shadows and hug the brittle old Count.

"Kiss me, Father!" he cried.

The hug was too much for the dying vampire. His ribcage cracked. With his last breath he said, "Don't ... squeeze ... please ..."

Then Smirk was holding not a vampire father but two armfuls of old dust. He opened his arms and the dust fell to the floor. Shocked as he was, he stepped back into the shadows before the sun destroyed him too.

Wilfred wiped away a tear. "If you are my father's real son," he said, "who am I?"

"You," Smirk said, "are the only son of Dweeb van Helsing, the man I called Papa – or Misery Guts, depending on my mood."

"But he's dead too," Wilfred said. "I'll never even meet him."

"Not unless you dig him up," Smirk replied. "But you have the farm."

"Farm?" Wilfred said.

"I inherited it when Mama and Papa died. It's a mess because I never wanted to be a farmer, but you're welcome to it. I suppose I'd better move in here and become the new Count Dracula. Er ... you don't mind, do you?"

"Mind?" Wilfred cried. "This is wonderful! I'm not a vampire. Or a wimpire. I'm a Boring Normal!"

"And I," Smirk said, "can stop feeling bad about not working in the fields and milking the rotten cows."

"You have cows?" Wilfred said in wonder.

"Five," Smirk said.

"Then I can have fresh milk every morning."

"You can have it till it pours out of your ears," Smirk replied. "And I, at last, can drink blood."

"Will we have to swap names too?" Wilfred said.

"Let's not," Smirk said. "I don't see myself as a Wilfred somehow."

With these important matters settled, they fetched a broom and swept the dust of the dead Count into an empty biscuit tin. Smirk put the tin on a shelf in the dining room and vowed never to put biscuits in it.

Then Wilfred van Helsing, farmer's son, left Castle Dracula for ever. He sang a cheery song and there was a spring in his step as he strolled down Bram Hill. Ahead of him lay the life he'd always dreamed of. A normal life, in which he could lie about in the sun all day, and sleep all night long.

Oh yes, and not feel bad about preferring milk fresh from the cow to blood fresh from the neck.

Our books are tested
for children and young people by
children and young people.

Thanks to everyone who consulted on
a manuscript for their time and effort in
helping us to make our books better
for our readers.